Rhymes

Written by Annemarie Young,
based on the original characters
created by Roderick Hunt and Alex Brychta
Illustrated by Alex Brychta

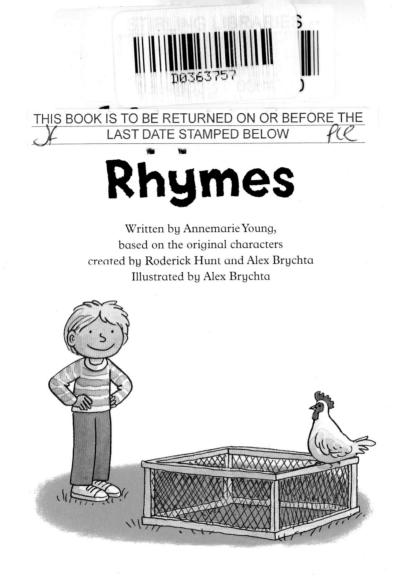

OXFORD
UNIVERSITY PRESS

Read these rhyming words and
find them in the picture.

A bug in a mug.

A jug on the rug.

What else can you
find in the picture that
rhymes with **mug**?

hug, slug

21

Maze haze

Help Dad get home in the fog.

Read these rhyming words and
find them in the picture.

A wet pet!

A fan and a can.

What other things
can you find in the
picture that rhyme with
pet and **can**?

jet, net, man, pan

Read these rhyming words and find them in the picture.

Less mess, Biff!

Ted is on the bed.

What things can you find in the picture that rhyme with **sock**?

clock, rock

Read these rhyming words and
find them in the picture.

Hop to the top.

Bill is on the hill.

What else can you
find in the picture that
rhymes with **top**?

mop, pop

Read these rhyming words and
find them in the picture.

A dog on a log.

Huff and puff!

What else can you
find in the picture that
rhymes with **dog**?

fog, jog, bog

Read these rhyming words and
find them in the picture.

Jack and his backpack.

Mack in a sack.

What else can you
find in the picture that
rhymes with **sack**?

track

15

Read these rhyming words and
find them in the picture.

The hen is in a pen.

The egg is on
a peg.

What else can you
find in the picture that
rhymes with **pen**
and **peg**?

ten, men, leg

Read these rhyming words and find them in the picture.

A ticket in a pocket.

A rocket in a bucket.

What else can you find in the picture that rhymes with **duck**?

truck

19

Read these rhyming words and
find them in the picture.

Pat a cat.

A rat sat on a mat.

What else can you
find in the picture that
rhymes with **cat**?

hat, bat